Filbert
the Good Little Fiend

*For little fiends
and angels everywhere*

H.O.

First published 2013 by Walker Books Ltd, 87 Vauxhall Walk, London SE11 5HJ • This edition published 2014
• Text © 2013 Hiawyn Oram • Illustrations © 2013 Jimmy Liao • The right of Hiawyn Oram and Jimmy Liao
to be identified as author and illustrator respectively of this work has been asserted by them in accordance
with the Copyright, Designs and Patents Act 1988 • This book has been typeset in ITC Officina Serif •
Printed in China • All rights reserved. No part of this book may be reproduced, transmitted or stored
in an information retrieval system in any form or by any means, graphic, electronic or mechanical,
including photocopying, taping and recording, without prior written permission from the publisher.
• British Library Cataloguing in Publication Data: a catalogue record for this book is available
from the British Library • ISBN 978-1-4063-5269-6 • **www.walker.co.uk** • 10 9 8 7 6 5 4 3 2 1

Filbert
the
Good Little Fiend

Hiawyn Oram   Jimmy Liao

WALKER BOOKS
AND SUBSIDIARIES
LONDON · BOSTON · SYDNEY · AUCKLAND

There was
Daddy Fiend who was
FEROCIOUSLY fiendish.

There was Mummy Fiend
who was FIERCELY fiendish.

And there was Filbert,
their little fiend,
who was good,
good, GOOD.

"What's the matter with him?" said Daddy Fiend,
fiercely. "He won't say BOO to a goose,
MOO to a moose or PANTS to an ant.
He's no little fiend of mine!"

"You're right," wailed Mummy Fiend, as she helped Filbert
into his fiery red coat, horrifying horns and monstrous mittens.
"Now," she said, "we're all going out to be gruesome and ghastly –
you, your daddy and me."

But Filbert wouldn't be
those things. He wouldn't HUFF
or PUFF, TRAMPLE or TERRIFY,
GLARE or SCARE, ROAR
or HOLLER – or be one bit
BOTHERSOME and
BEASTLY.

Instead,
he helped to pick up
an old lady's dropped
shopping and then
he did some
birdwatching.

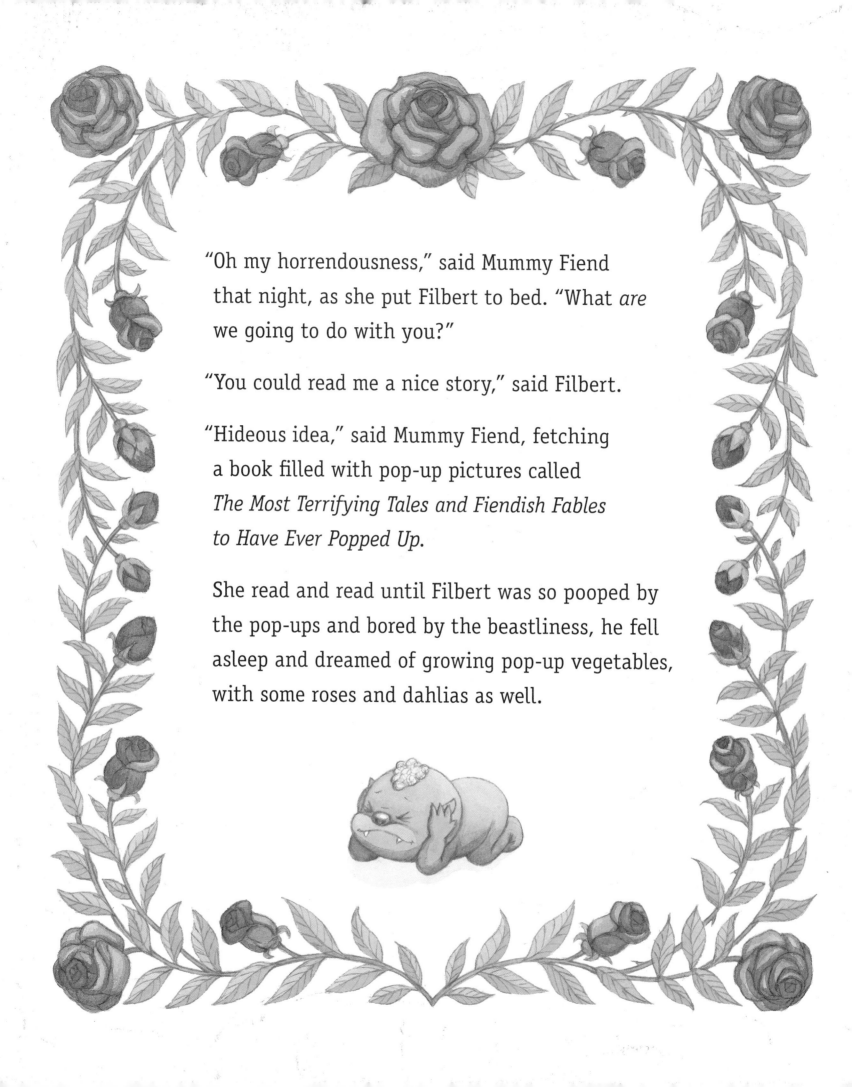

"Oh my horrendousness," said Mummy Fiend
that night, as she put Filbert to bed. "What *are*
we going to do with you?"

"You could read me a nice story," said Filbert.

"Hideous idea," said Mummy Fiend, fetching
a book filled with pop-up pictures called
*The Most Terrifying Tales and Fiendish Fables
to Have Ever Popped Up.*

She read and read until Filbert was so pooped by
the pop-ups and bored by the beastliness, he fell
asleep and dreamed of growing pop-up vegetables,
with some roses and dahlias as well.

The next day, as it happened, was the very day Filbert was to start school. Mummy and Daddy Fiend dropped him off, saying, "Now be a proper little fiend for us, *promise* you will?"

But Filbert didn't even nod.

He listened to Miss Fearsome-Frizz, his teacher, when she said, "Get ready for Musical Thumps!" and "All on the mat for Shriek and Show and after that we'll have a Purple Paint Fight!"

But Filbert didn't join in.

Instead, he built an aeroplane out of drinking straws. He played cat's cradle in a corner – very quietly – and he hid in the Little Fiends' loos for the whole of the Purple Paint Fight.

When he came back, Miss Fearsome-Frizz looked at him suspiciously. "Filbert! You've been *keeping out of the fight*, haven't you?"

"Yes," said Filbert, who never lied because he didn't see the need to.

"Well, I *can't* have such good behaviour in my class," Miss Fearsome-Frizz sizzled. "You will go and sit outside on the grassy Good Step until you've decided to behave like a *proper* little fiend."

So Filbert put on his coat, his horns
and his mittens and ran outside to the
grassy Good Step, where he watched
the clouds drifting by and the flowers
nodding in the breeze.

Then suddenly, out of nowhere,
came a little angel shape – actually a little angel –
flying so fast and furiously that she wasn't looking
where she was going and ...

BUMP!

She bumped into
the tree and landed in
a heap beside Filbert.

"Hello," said Filbert. "I'm Filbert."

"Hello," said the little angel heap. "I'm Florinda.
I've been sent out from Angel School for *not* being good enough.
And I'm *very* furious about it."

"And I've been sent out from Fiend School for being *too* good,"
said Filbert. "And I'm thinking about it."

"Well, I wish you'd think of a good way to make
them happy with us *just as we are*!"
flounced Florinda.

"Hmm..."
said Filbert, jumping up.
"I think I have.
Here we go!"

Then, Filbert took off
his fiery red coat,
his horrifying horns
and his monstrous mittens
and lent them to Florinda.

Florinda took off
her soft silvery cloak,
her fluffy white wings
and her golden halo
and lent them to Filbert.

So, when Florinda walked into Angel School looking like
a right little fiend, everyone *begged* her to get back to
being nothing worse than a *not* quite perfect little angel.

And when Filbert walked into Fiend School looking like
a proper little angel, everyone *begged* him to get back
to being nothing better than a *good* little fiend.

After that, the angels in Angel School sighed and accepted there was one among them who wasn't perfect.

Miss Fearsome-Frizz kept her hair on when Filbert was good. "At least he's no angel!" she muttered to herself.

And Filbert's daddy and mummy let him be his good self without complaining once. (Though they did have another baby fiend rather quickly in the hope they'd get something gruesome and ghastly ... and it has to be said they weren't disappointed.)

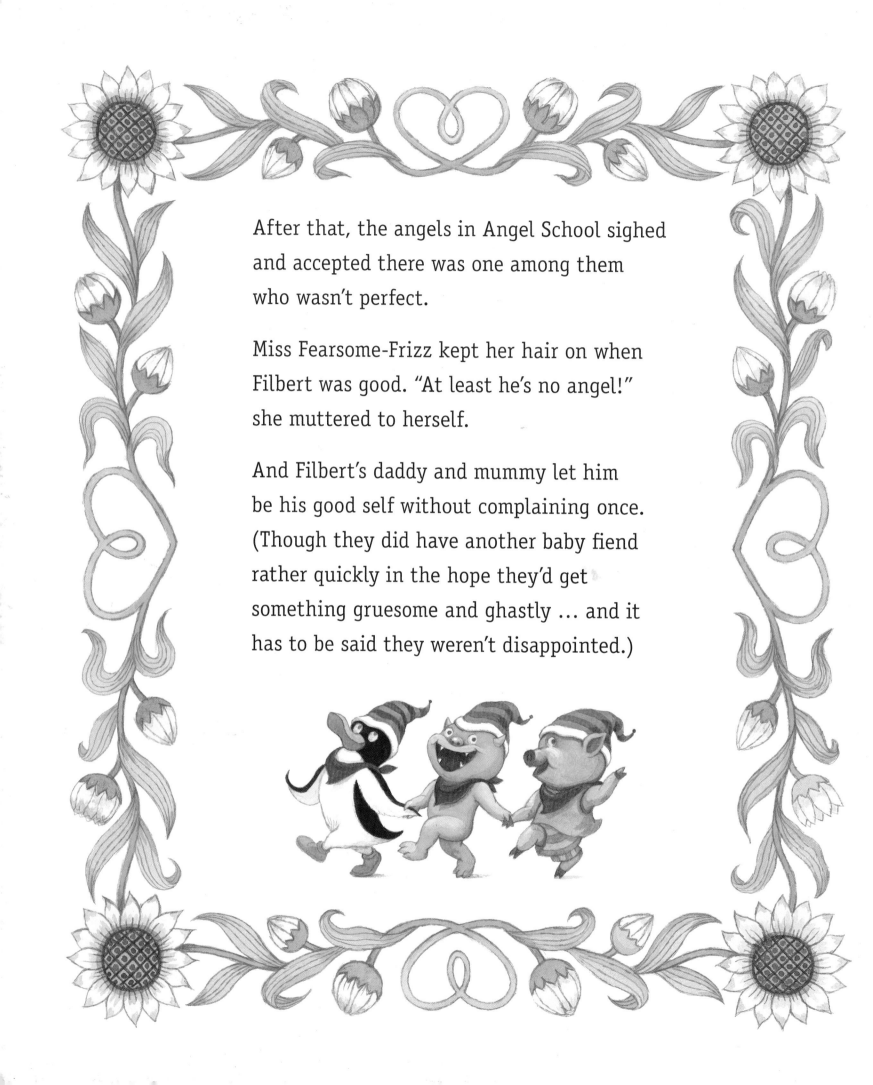

As for Filbert and Florinda,
well ... you can guess what happened to them.
They became the firmest friends ever.
Why? You know why.

Because together they were just about
AS GOOD AS IT GETS ...

a *not* quite perfect little angel and ...
an *almost* angelical little fiend.